Dustin!

Wishing you a stellar
journey!

Peter H Reynolds 2009

The North Star

Written and Illustrated by
Peter H. Reynolds

FABLE VISION PRESS

The North Star
CLASSIC EDITION

PUBLISHED BY

Fable Vision Press
308 CONGRESS ST. BOSTON, MA 02210

Seventh Printing
ISBN-10: 1-891405-00-4
ISBN-13: 978-1-891405-006
Library of Congress Catalog no. 9794615

PRINTED IN HONG KONG

To order additional books, or the North Star Classroom Guide,
or the North Star Musical, please visit

WWW.PETERHREYNOLDS.COM   WWW.FABLEVISION.COM   WWW.DEDHAMBLUEBUNNY.COM

dedicated
to all the parents
and teachers of the
w   o   r   l   d
and those who are
brave enough to
follow their
d   r   e   a   m   s.

A
sweet
breeze met the
boy as he awoke
to his

journey.

He travelled on all fours
for quite sometime ...

And he grew.

And he paused.

One day he had the
urge to stand...
to walk.

It made his
journey easier...

He was soon
inspired to learn
how to run.

But for the most
Part he walked.

He wasn't afraid of
much.

He wandered the fields
exploring, sometimes stopping

Sometimes going happily
in circles... sometimes

d a n c i n g.

Sometimes napping.

One day the boy saw
an oak leaf drift and
land on the water.

He was curious
how the leaf managed
to float...

... the way the
stars seemed to
float in the night
sky.

A spray of sand
interrupted his thoughts.

"Where are you going
in such a hurry?"

But the rabbit
shot out of sight,
disappearing into a
path he had never
noticed before.

He left the
floating leaf and
wandered toward
the path...

...and there
he saw a cat.

The cat purrrred gently.

The boy asked...

"Where did the rabbit go in such a hurry?"

"She was in a rush to start her journey. It's time for you to start your journey too."

The cat purrrred deeply.

"Oh, but I _have_ been on a journey! I've seen many wonderful things.

Some I understand and some I don't...

like how that leaf floats on the water..."

Well, that's fascinating,
but I'd hate for you
to be late.

You don't
want to be
left
behind. "

"Behind? Who's
a head of me?"

"You wouldn't be<u>lieve</u>
how many!
You know, you're not
the only one on
this journey."

"Plenty ahead of you.
Lots to follow."

He began walking
down the path.

It stretched
out
far ahead
of him.

Signs kept pointing him along the way.

Some parts of the journey
were easy

Although he was following the well-worn path,

he had a growing feeling that he was lost.

THIS WAY

The forest
seemed to be
growing thicker
and the soil was
wet and muddy.

Clouds had
rolled in overhead
making everything
dark.

It swirled on a breeze and was carried deep into the forest...

...it disappeared behind a grove of trees.

The boy found
the leaf floating on
a pond in a peaceful
c l e a r i n g.

It looked like
a delicate boat
on a dreamy
voyage.

His gaze was
interrupted by
a VOICE...

The muddy ground became covered with water.
He could no longer see a clear path.

He sloshed through the swamp the best he could.

...a bird.

The boy marveled
at the bird's brilliant
feathers. He remembered
how he had once seen
a feather floating near
his beach.

I don't think so.
I mean, I'm not
sure if I'm lost. I
really hadn't thought
about it.'

I've been
following
the path.

It seems like many
people have taken
it before me...

...and there have
been many signs
along the way...

And a
very helpful
cat guided me
back to the path
when I tried
to
wander.

the crickets fell
s i l e n t
as the bird asked...

"But where is
it that you
want to Be?"

I'm not sure,
but I know
this
is not the
place I want
to be.

Ask yourself where
is it you want to go and
then follow the signs you
already know.

What signs?
Where are they?

He was upset
that the bird
had flown away
into the cLoupy
night sky.

He stared skyward
trying to see where
the bird had
gone.

And as he did
the clouds seemed to
melt... revealing the
inky black sky... and
there above him...

...was a
Star,
a very
bright
star.

He stared at the star
and felt a whisper in
his ear, a pang in his heart,
a tingling in his spine.
He could hear the star.
The voice sounded so
f a m i l i a r.

He began to go in the direction of the star. Many other stars soon appeared in the dark velvet sky.

This WAY

All the stars
s t r e t c h e d
out above him, guiding
him like a great big
map as he navigated
out of the swamp.

THIS
WAY

He stopped and
rested a moment
and noticed something
appear in the stars.

His gaze was interrupted by
a deep voice coming from
behind him.

"What are you staring at?"
the voice croaked.

It was a frog.
"What is up there? What
is so interesting?"

The boy waded closer
and answered, "Stars.
I'm looking at the stars."

"What stars?" The frog
was puzzled. "I see a
dark sky and mist and
low green clouds."

"You don't see
them?"

"They are helping me
guide myself out of
this swamp."

"Would you like
to come with me?

"No thankyou. I am quite at home here. I swam here as a tadpole and grew up here. Here I will stay."

The boy realized at
that moment that everyone
has a different voyage,
different signs,

their own stars, their
own constellations.

The boy left
the frog who
was smiling
broadly.

Suddenly...
he heard a cry.
It was coming
from the center of the
deep river running
into the swamp.

It was the rabbit
who had been in such a
h u r r y.

She looked hungry and
very tired.

The boy waded out but realized the river was too deep. The rabbit was trapped.

He saw an oak leaf drift by. It gave him an idea.

The boy looked up and noticed that the star had become even brighter.

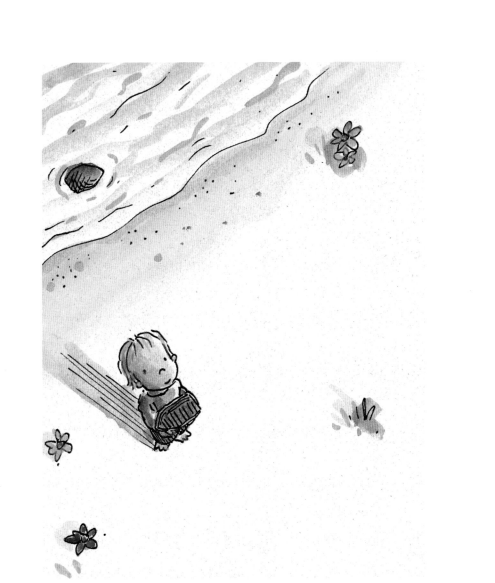

He followed the star and
as he did the muddy ground
grew drier... then grassy...
then soft and sandy.

Finally he came to a rest atop a dune and there below him was a beach...

... and a boat.

He gazed out
into the ocean
and he saw the
s t a r.

The star glowed patiently reminding him that it was still a long journey ahead but it was his own journey, his very own wonderful journey.

The
Beginning